Layla   Jayden   Caleb

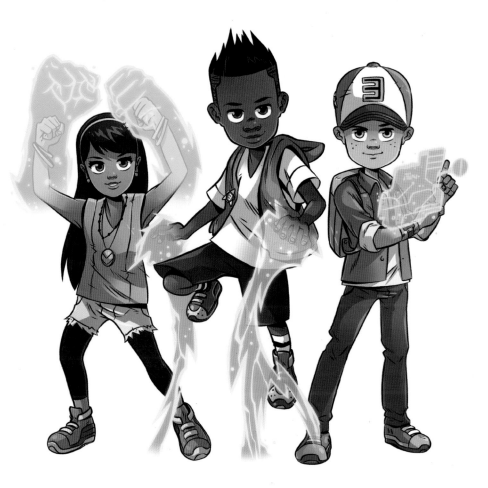

They are…

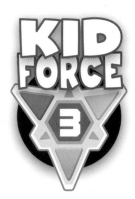

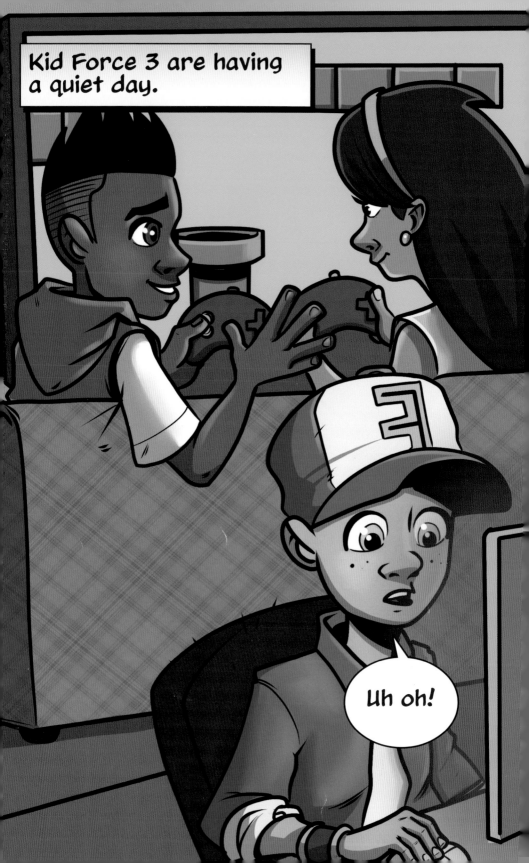

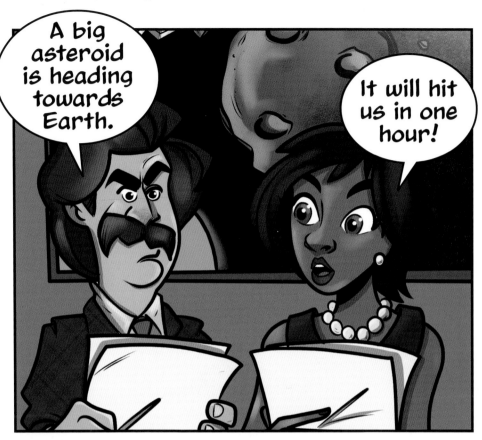

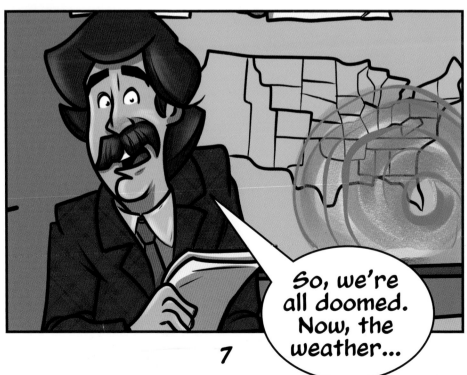

7

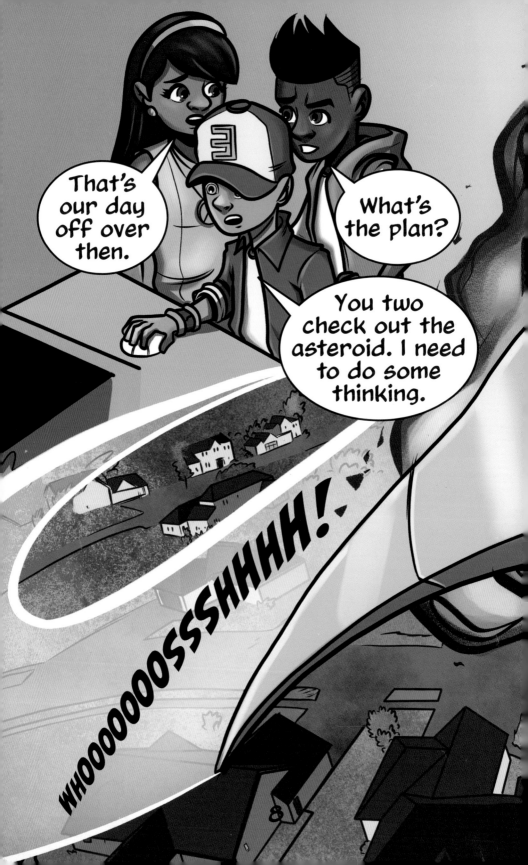

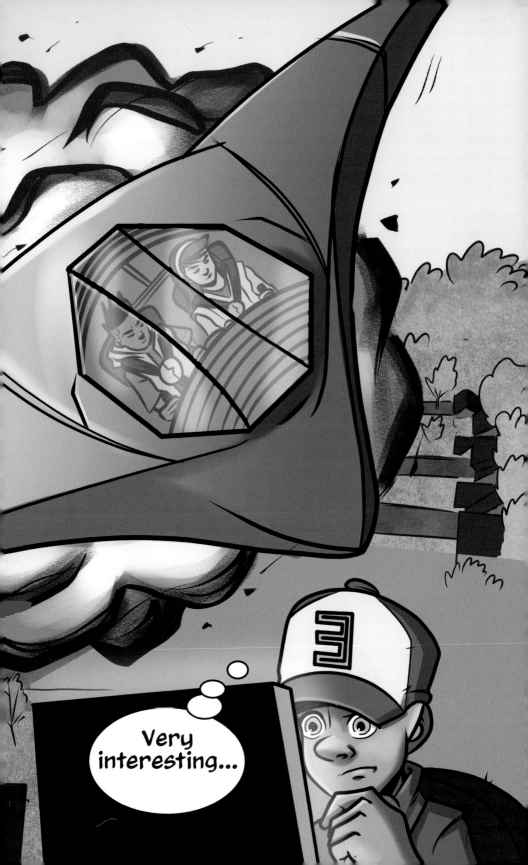

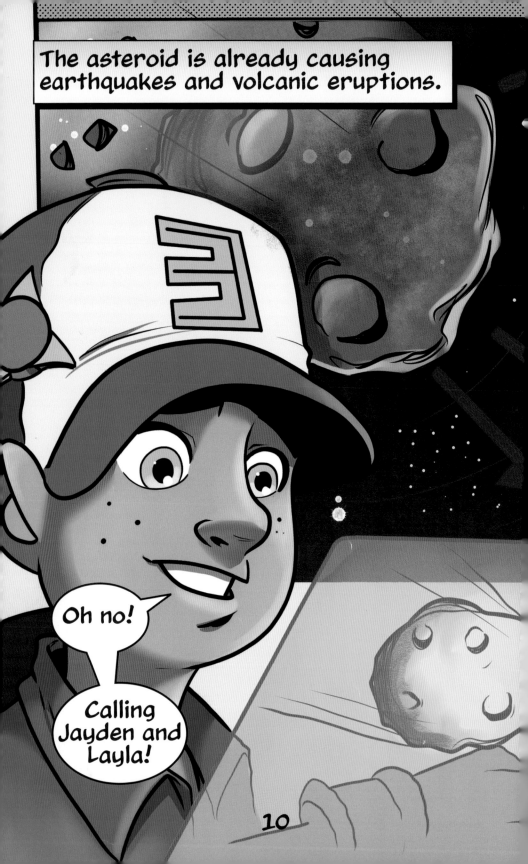

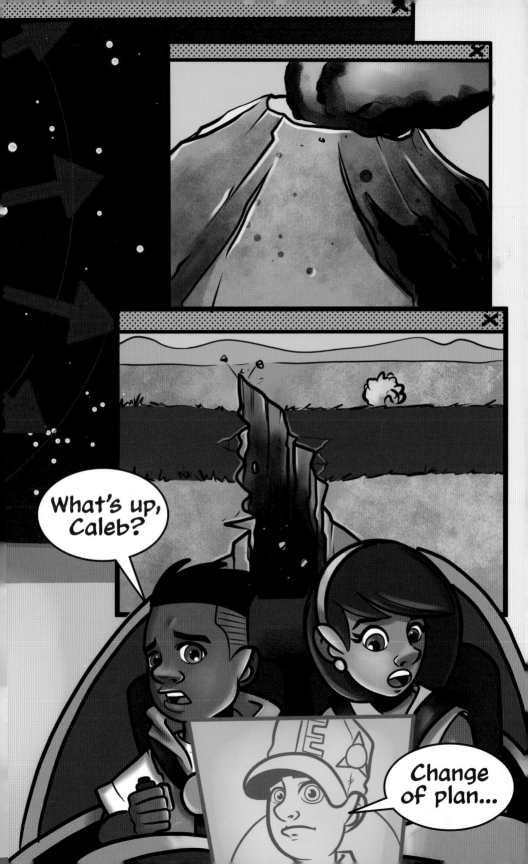

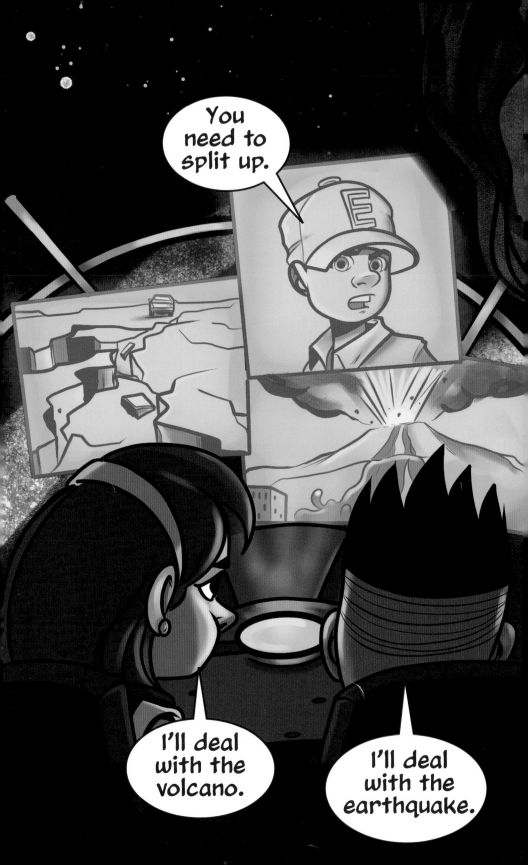

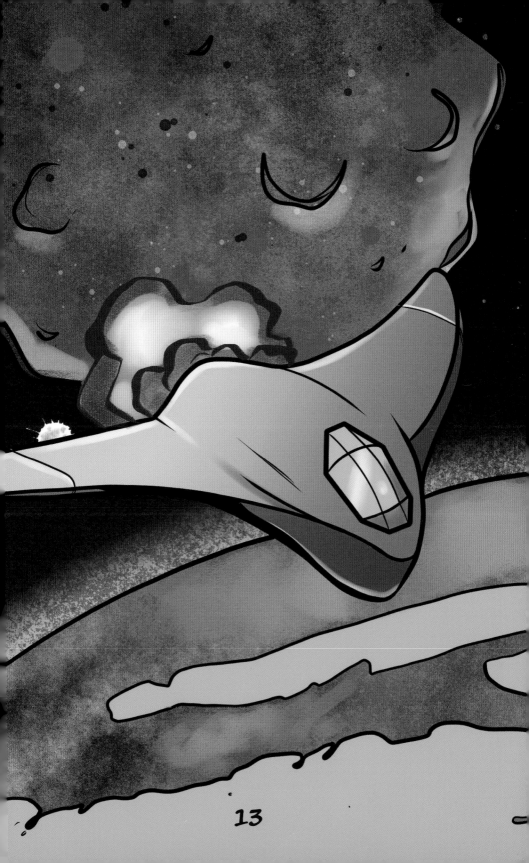

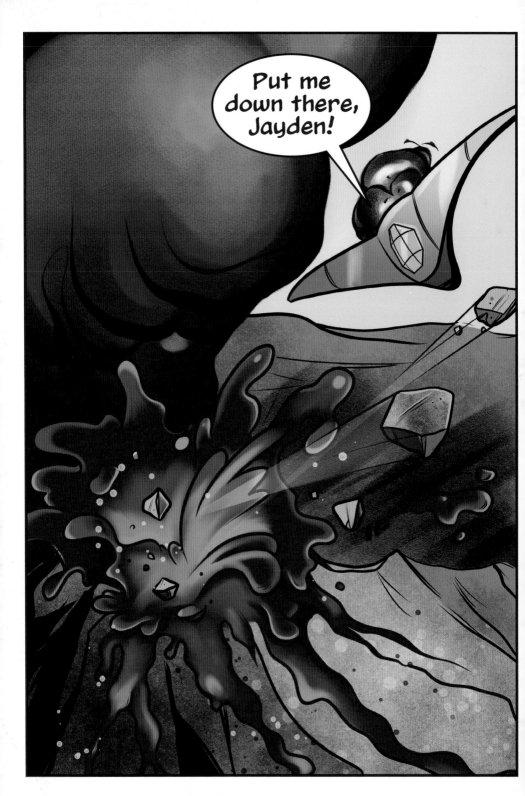

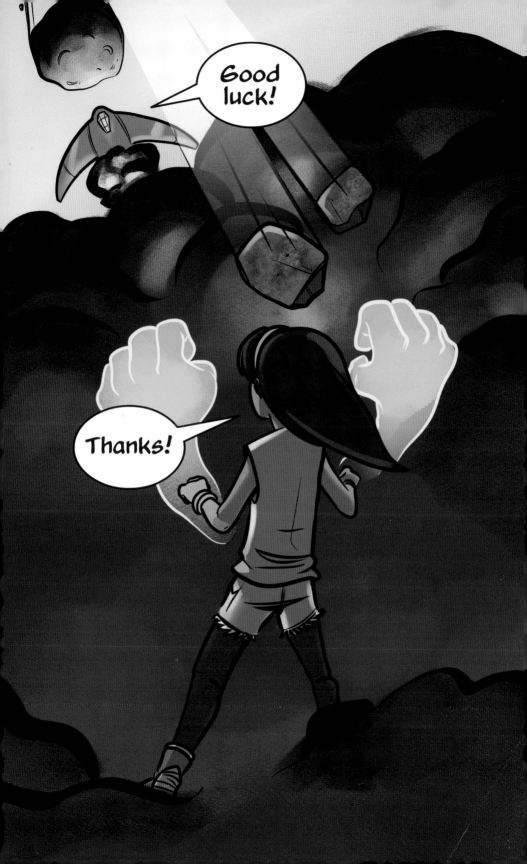

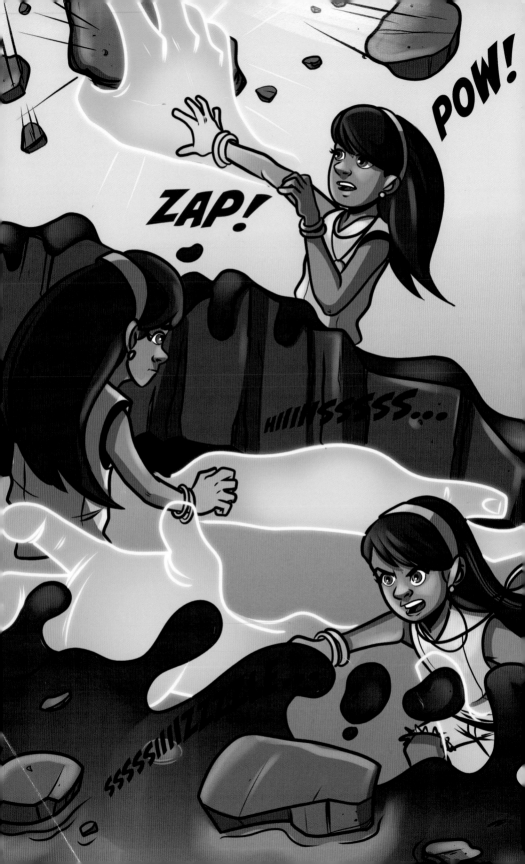

Layla battles the volcano but nothing seems to work.

She is running out of ideas.

"This isn't working!" said Layla.
"Any ideas, Caleb?"

"Try plugging it!" shouted Caleb.

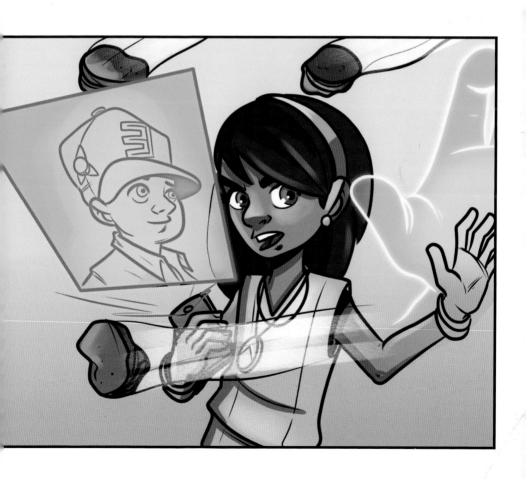

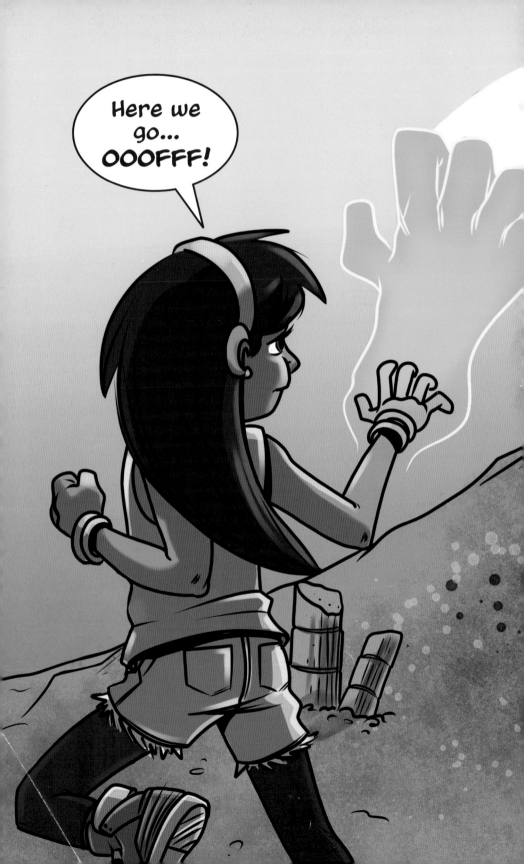

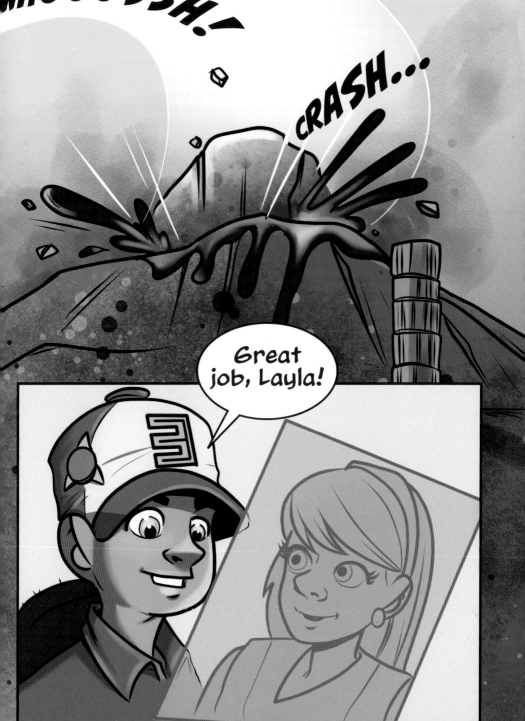

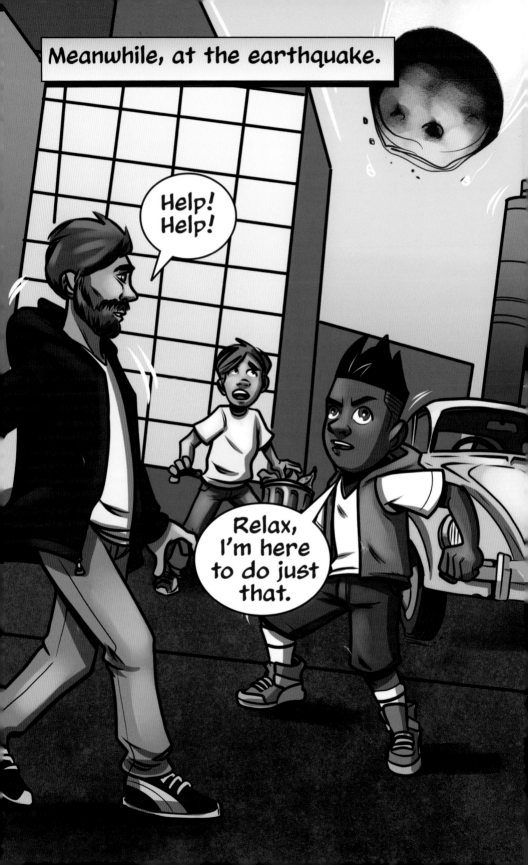

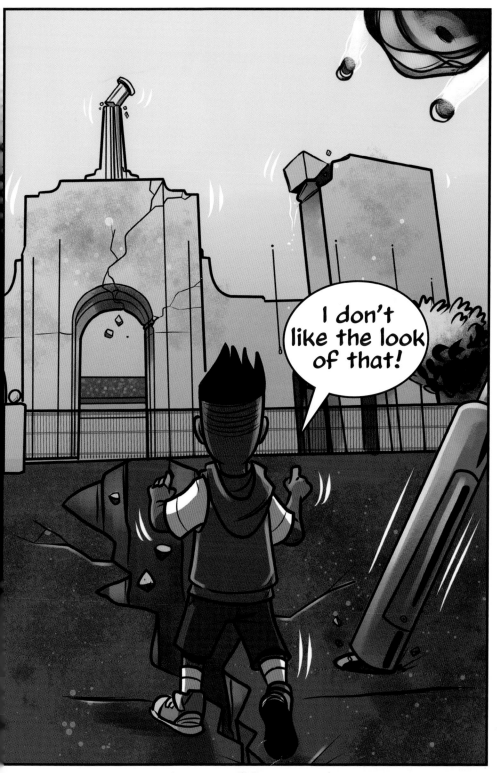

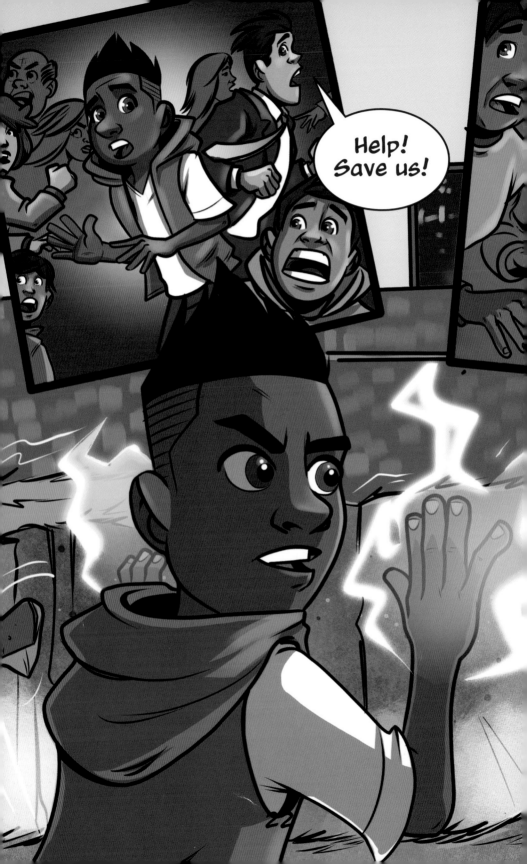

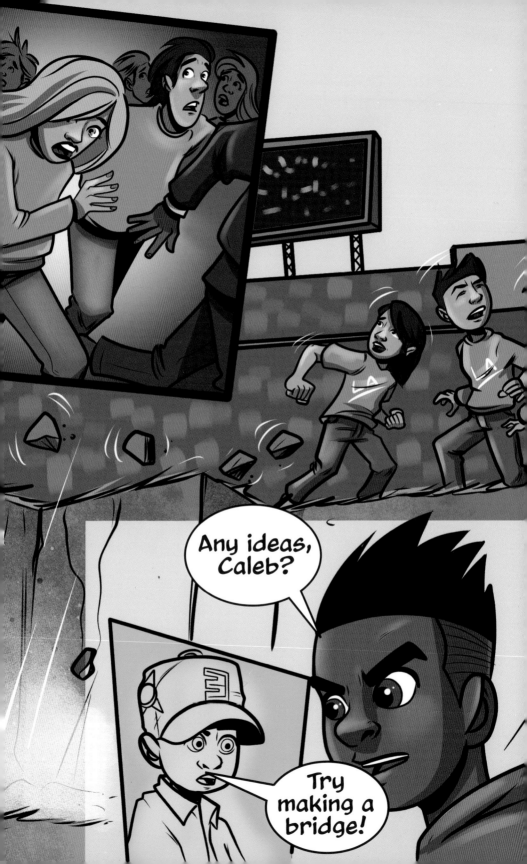

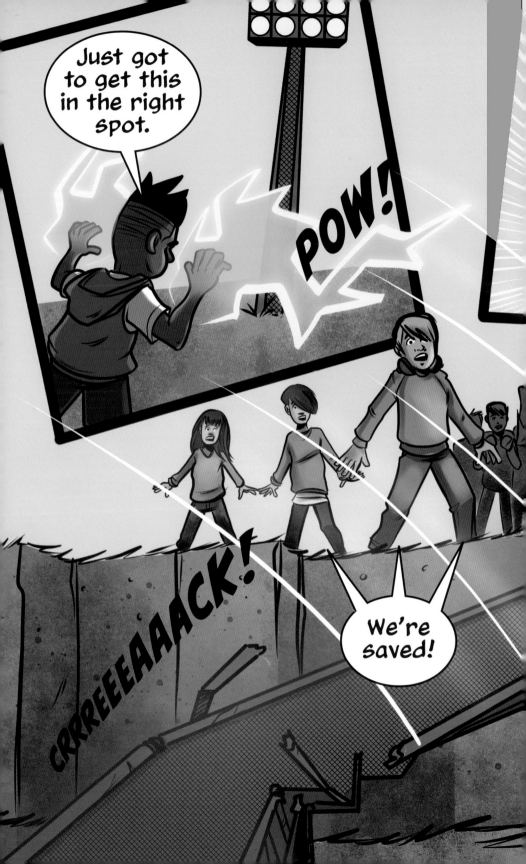

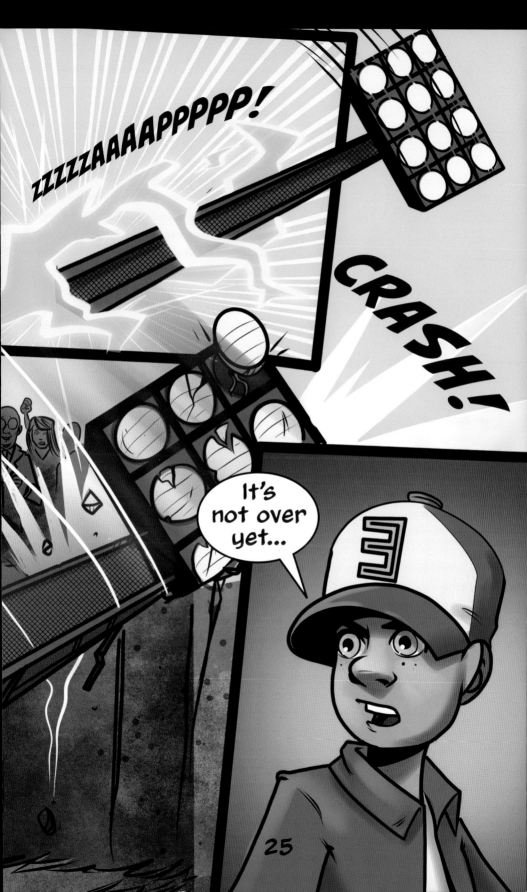

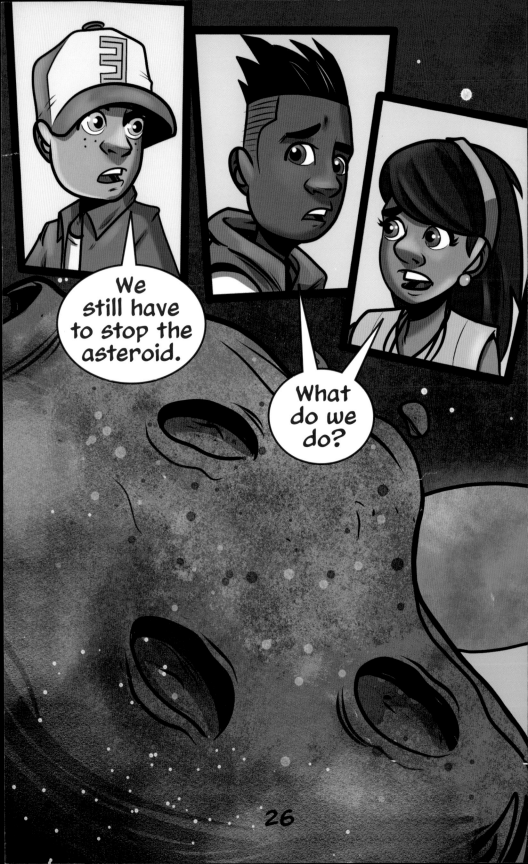

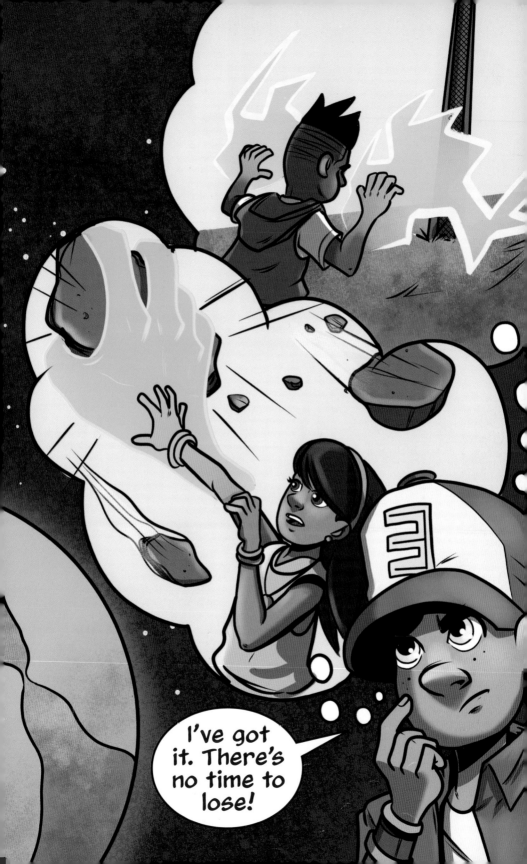

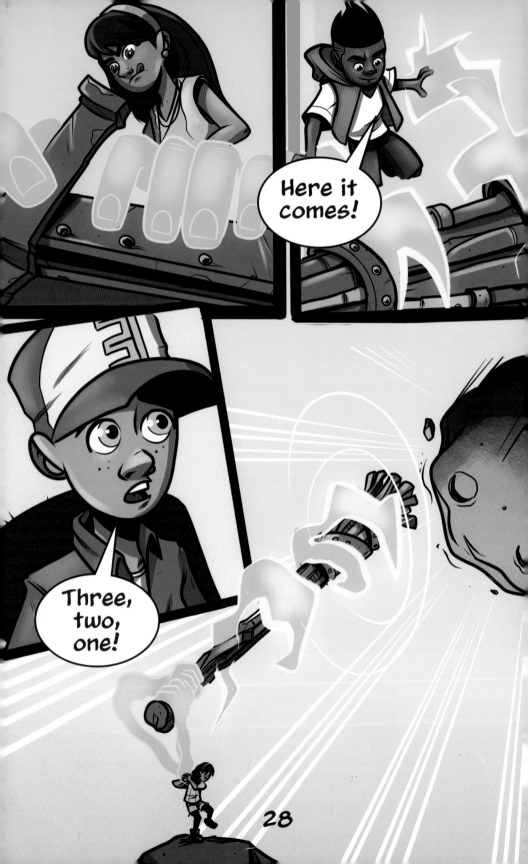

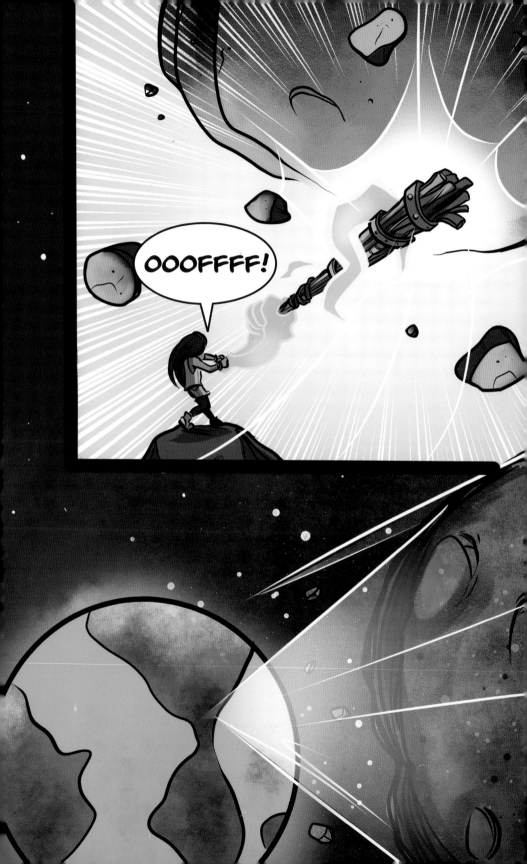

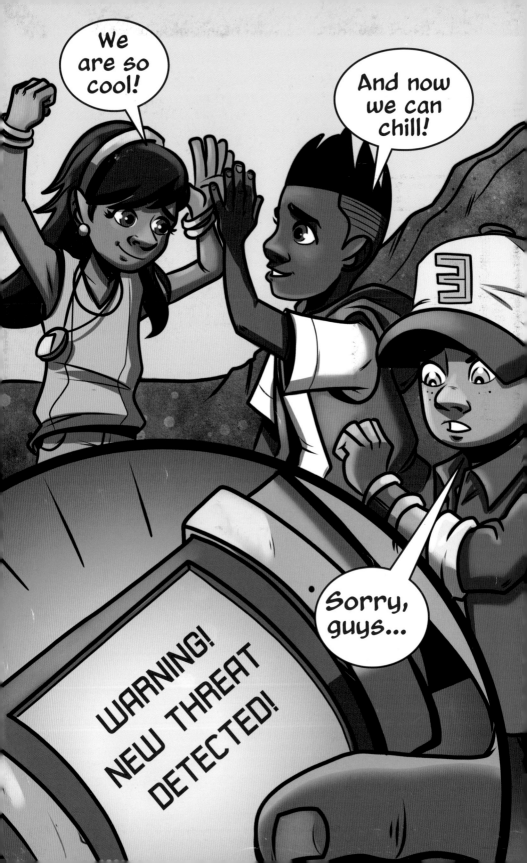